THE BIRTHDAY SURPRISE

BY LEIGH STEPHENS

ILLUSTRATIONS BY ARTFUL DOODLERS

SCHOLASTIC INC.

ISBN 978-1-338-15901-1

10 9 8 7 6 5 4 3 2 1 17 18 19 20 21

Printed in the U.S.A. 40
First printing 2017

Book design by Erin McMahon

“It’s Pam Cake’s birthday!” Rainbow Kate told the Shoppies. She wanted to throw Pam Cake a surprise party.

“I love parties!” said Bubbleisha.

“I love surprises!” said Donatina.

Jessicake knew the perfect spot for the party: the Cupcake Queen Café!

"I'll bake the yummiest birthday cupcakes!" she said.

Bubbleisha was in charge of decorations.

"Hmm," she said, looking around the café. "How many balloons do you think we can we fit in here?"

Donatina said she would plan the party games.

She started making a list of all her ideas.

“I’ll find Pam Cake,” said Peppa-Mint. She would make sure the birthday girl stayed away from the café.

“How will you keep her busy all day?” asked Donatina.

“Shopping, of course!” said Peppa-Mint.

Rayne-Bow and Raylene Rainbow came into the café with Strawberry Kiss and Sneaky Wedge.

"Cupcake time!" said Raylene Rainbow.

"What's going on?" asked Rayne-Bow when she saw the Shoppies hard at work.

"We're planning a surprise party for Pam Cake," said Rainbow Kate.

Sneaky Wedge bounced up and down. "Party is my middle name!" she said.

The Shopkins wanted to help.

Bubbleisha and Rayne-Bow went to the party store for decorations. They found bouncy balloons, sparkly streamers, and colorful confetti.

“Pam Cake will love these balloons!” said Bubbleisha.

Just then, the wind blew. “Ah!” cried Rayne-Bow.

Luckily, Bubbleisha grabbed her and the balloons just in time.

When Bubbleisha and Rayne-Bow got back to the café, Rainbow Kate frowned.

"These are all pink!" she said.

"I know! Aren't they pretty?" said Bubbleisha.

“Yes, but the party has a rainbow theme,” said Rainbow Kate. She held up the rainbow invitations she was making.

“Pam Cake loves pink!” said Bubbleisha.

“You love pink, Bubbleisha,” said Rainbow Kate.

In the kitchen, Jessicake was baking Pam Cake's favorite cupcakes. Strawberry Kiss was helping.

"Maple syrup, please!" Jessicake said. Strawberry Kiss poured a cup of maple syrup into the batter.

“Brown sugar!” called Jessicake.

But instead of brown sugar, Strawberry Kiss dumped a bowl of strawberries into the mix.

"Strawberry Kiss! I said brown sugar, not berries!" said Jessicake.

"Cupcakes are always better with berries," said Strawberry Kiss.

“Maybe some kinds, but not Maple Sugar cupcakes,” said Jessicake with a sigh. “They’re Pam Cake’s favorite, and now they’re ruined!”

“I thought berry cupcakes were Pam Cake’s favorite,” said Strawberry Kiss.

“No, those are *your* favorite,” replied Jessicake.

In the front of the café, Donatina and Sneaky Wedge were setting up party games.

Donatina hung a game of Pin the Frosting on the Cupcake.

"A little to the left," said Sneaky Wedge.

The best game of all was Donatina's "Donut-O-Fun." It was a box shaped like a donut and filled with candy!

"Can I have just one piece of candy now?" asked Sneaky Wedge.

"Not yet," said Donatina. "The candy is sealed inside and the glue needs to dry. Don't touch it!"

Across the room, Rainbow Kate tried to convince Bubbleisha to change the party decorations.

"The pink balloons don't match the rainbow invitations!" said Rainbow Kate. "Right, Donatina?"

Donatina went over to help.

Sneaky Wedge really wanted a piece of candy. She spotted a piece sticking out the side of the Donut-O-Fun.

She looked around to see if anyone was watching.

Sneaky Wedge peered into the kitchen. Jessicake was trying to pick the berries out of her Maple Sugar cupcake batter. Strawberry Kiss kept sneaking more berries in.

"There are just too many!" Jessicake cried.

With everyone so busy, Sneaky Wedge spotted her chance. She stood beneath the donut where the piece of candy was sticking out. Then she jumped.

She grabbed the candy wrapper, but it didn't move.

So she tugged.

And tugged.

And tugged some more.

Meanwhile, Pam Cake was shopping with Peppa-Mint.

"Let's go to the Cupcake Queen Café," said Pam Cake.

"Can we go to one more store?" asked Peppa-Mint. She couldn't let Pam Cake near the café yet!

"But, we've been shopping for hours!" said Pam Cake. "Come on, my treat!"

In the café, Sneaky Wedge gave the piece of candy one last tug and—*POP!*

The Donut-O-Fun exploded. Candy went everywhere!

“My donut!” cried Donatina.
“My cupcakes!” said Jessicake.
“My decorations!” said Bubbleisha.
“My party!” cried Rainbow Kate.

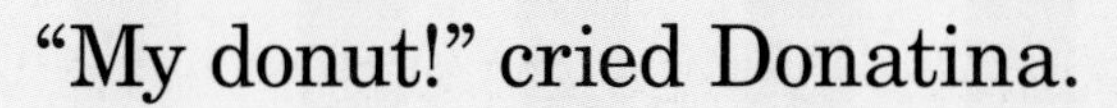

Just then, the door to the café opened. Pam Cake walked in.

"Wow!" she said. "What's going on?"

"Oh, Pam Cake!" Rainbow Kate cried. "We wanted to throw you the best surprise party ever. But the decorations don't match. The cupcakes are ruined. And there's candy everywhere. I'm so sorry!"

"I love it!" said Pam Cake, looking around the café. "I can tell that you picked out these decorations, Bubbleisha. Jessicake, those Maple Berry cupcakes look yummy! And I can't wait to race to pick up all this candy. Great game, Donatina!

“You each gave the party your own personal style. And you brought it all together, Rainbow Kate. Thank you!” said Pam Cake.

Rainbow Kate was thrilled when Pam Cake gave her a big hug.

“Surprise! This is the best party ever!” said Sneaky Wedge.

Dear Family and Friends of New Readers,

Welcome to Scholastic Reader. We have taken over ninety years' worth of experience with teachers, parents, and children and put it into a program that is designed to match your child's interest and skills. Each Scholastic Reader is designed to support your child's efforts to learn how to read at every age and every stage.

- First Reader
- Preschool – Kindergarten
- ABC's
- First words

- Beginning Reader
- Preschool – Grade 1
- Sight words
- Words to sound out
- Simple sentences

- Developing Reader
- Grades 1 – 2
- New vocabulary
- Longer sentences

- Growing Reader
- Grades 1 – 3
- Reading for inspiration and information

ring books with your new reader, please
.com. Enjoy helping your child learn to
d!

—Scholastic Inc.

SCHOLASTIC

Rainbow Kate wants to throw Pam Cake the sweetest birthday celebration ever. She asks the other Shoppies to help her plan a surprise party—but too many cooks spoil the cake! One thing is for sure: This will be a birthday Pam Cake will never forget!

ABC's & first words.

Sight words, words to sound out & simple sentences.

New vocabulary & longer sentences.

Reading for inspiration & information.

Based on the best research about how children learn to read, Scholastic Readers are developed under the supervision of reading experts and are educator approved.

SCHOLASTIC
scholastic.com

More leveling information for this book:
www.scholastic.com/readinglevel

$3.99 US / $5.50 C

ISBN 978-1-338-15901-1

We Speak the Word of the Lord

A Practical Plan for More Effective Preaching

Daniel E. Harris